SHOWDOWN ON THE SMUGGLER'S MOON: VOLUME 6

It is an era of renewed hope for the Rebellion. On his quest to learn the ways of the Jedi, Luke Skywalker has been taken prisoner on the infamous moon Nar Shaddaa by Jedi artifact collector GRAKKUS THE HUTT.

Forced into a fight to the death with Kongo the Disemboweler, Luke is struggling to survive. Unbeknownst to Grakkus, his Gamemaster has sold him out to the Empire. Meanwhile, Princess Leia, Han Solo, and Sana, the woman claiming to be Han's wife, are traveling to Nar Shaddaa in response to the distress call about Luke from the Rebel fleet.

Chewbacca and C-3PO, having arrived on the Smuggler's Moon first, encounter a bounty hunter named Dengar who plans to use Chewie as bait. Han arrives just in time to fight to reclaim his friend and continue the search for Luke....

JASON AARON
Writer

STUART IMMONEN
Artist

WADE VON GRAWBADGER
Inker

JUSTIN PONSOR
Colorist

CHRIS ELIOPOULOS
Letterer

IMMONEN, VON GRAWBADGER, PONSOR
Cover Artists

HEATHER ANTOS
Assistant Editor

JORDAN D. WHITE
Editor

C.B. CEBULSKI
Executive Editor

AXEL ALONSO
Editor In Chief

JOE QUESADA
Chief Creative Officer

DAN BUCKLEY
Publisher

For Lucasfilm:
Creative Director MICHAEL SIGLAIN
Senior Editor FRANK PARISI
Lucasfilm Story Group RAYNE ROBERTS, PABLO HIDALGO, LELAND CHEE

ABDO
Spotlight

ABDOPUBLISHING.COM

Reinforced library bound edition published in 2017 by Spotlight,
a division of ABDO, PO Box 398166, Minneapolis, Minnesota 55439.
Spotlight produces high-quality reinforced library bound editions for
schools and libraries. Published by agreement with Marvel Characters, Inc.

Printed in the United States of America, North Mankato, Minnesota.
092016
012017

 THIS BOOK CONTAINS
RECYCLED MATERIALS

marvelkids.com

STAR WARS © & TM 2016 LUCASFILM LTD.

PUBLISHER'S CATALOGING IN PUBLICATION DATA

Names: Aaron, Jason, author. | Bianchi, Simone ; Ponsor, Justin ; Immonen, Stuart ;
 Von Grawbadger, Wade, illustrators.
Title: Showdown on the Smuggler's Moon / writer: Jason Aaron ; art: Simone
 Bianchi ; Justin Ponsor ; Stuart Immomen ; Wade Von Grawbadger.
Description: Reinforced library bound edition. | Minneapolis, Minnesota : Spotlight,
 2017. | Series: Star Wars : Showdown on the Smuggler's Moon
Summary: After reading Ben Kenobi's journal, Luke Skywalker is imprisoned during
 his search for a Jedi Temple, while Han and Leia flee from some Imperial troops
 with help from an unexpected foe, and Chewbacca and C-3PO are attacked by
 a mysterious bounty hunter.
Identifiers: LCCN 2016941802 | ISBN 9781614795544 (volume 1) | ISBN
 9781614795551 (volume 2) | ISBN 9781614795568 (volume 3) | ISBN
 9781614795575 (volume 4) | ISBN 9781614795582 (volume 5) | ISBN
 9781614795599 (volume 6)
Subjects: LCSH: Star Wars fiction--Comic books, strips, etc.--Juvenile fiction. |
 Graphic novels--Juvenile fiction.
Classification: DDC 741.5--dc23
LC record available at https://lccn.loc.gov/2016941802

Spotlight

A Division of ABDO
abdopublishing.com

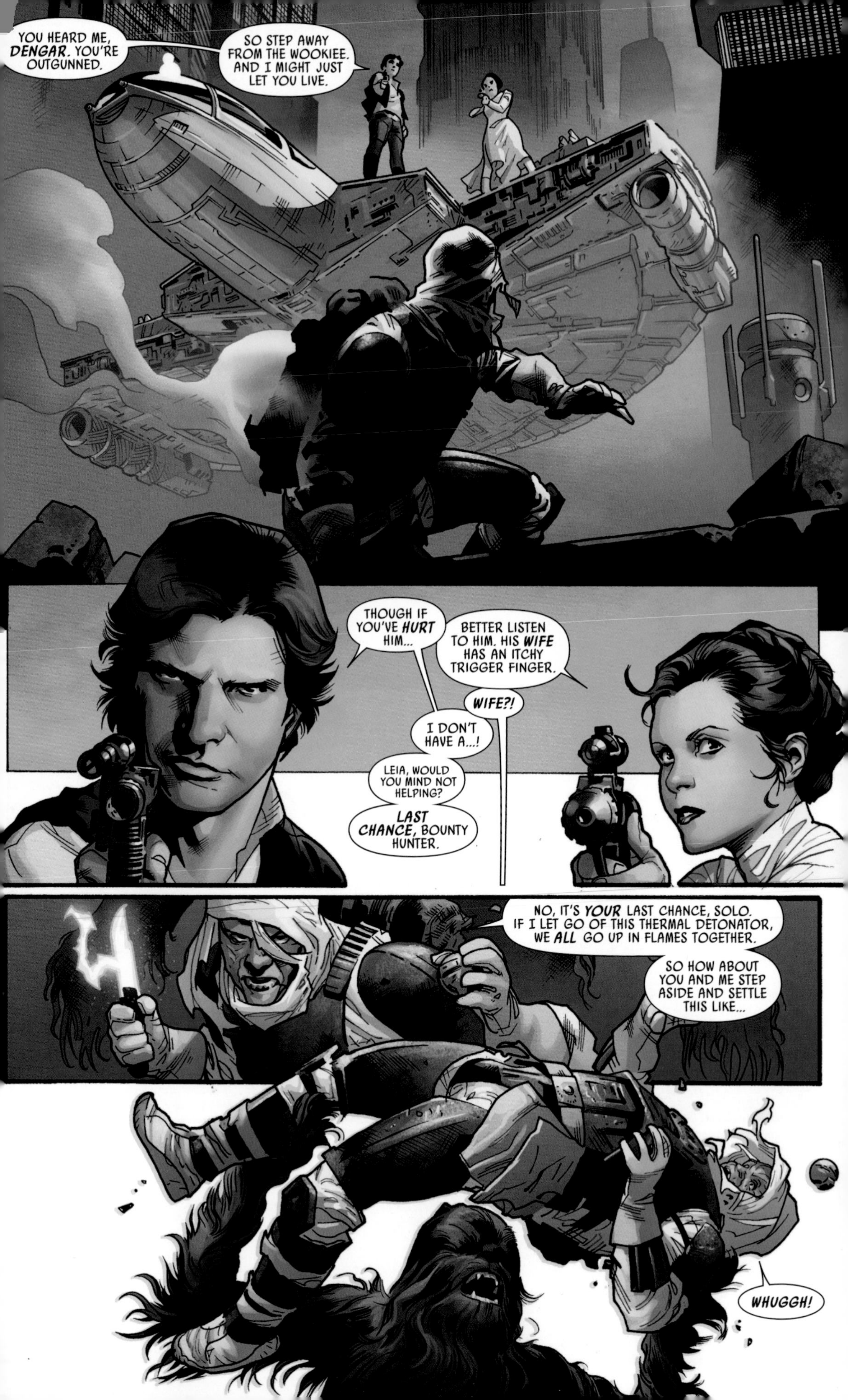
YOU HEARD ME, DENGAR. YOU'RE OUTGUNNED.
SO STEP AWAY FROM THE WOOKIEE. AND I MIGHT JUST LET YOU LIVE.
THOUGH IF YOU'VE HURT HIM...
BETTER LISTEN TO HIM. HIS WIFE HAS AN ITCHY TRIGGER FINGER.
WIFE?!
I DON'T HAVE A...!
LEIA, WOULD YOU MIND NOT HELPING?
LAST CHANCE, BOUNTY HUNTER.
NO, IT'S YOUR LAST CHANCE, SOLO. IF I LET GO OF THIS THERMAL DETONATOR, WE ALL GO UP IN FLAMES TOGETHER.
SO HOW ABOUT YOU AND ME STEP ASIDE AND SETTLE THIS LIKE...
WHUGGH!

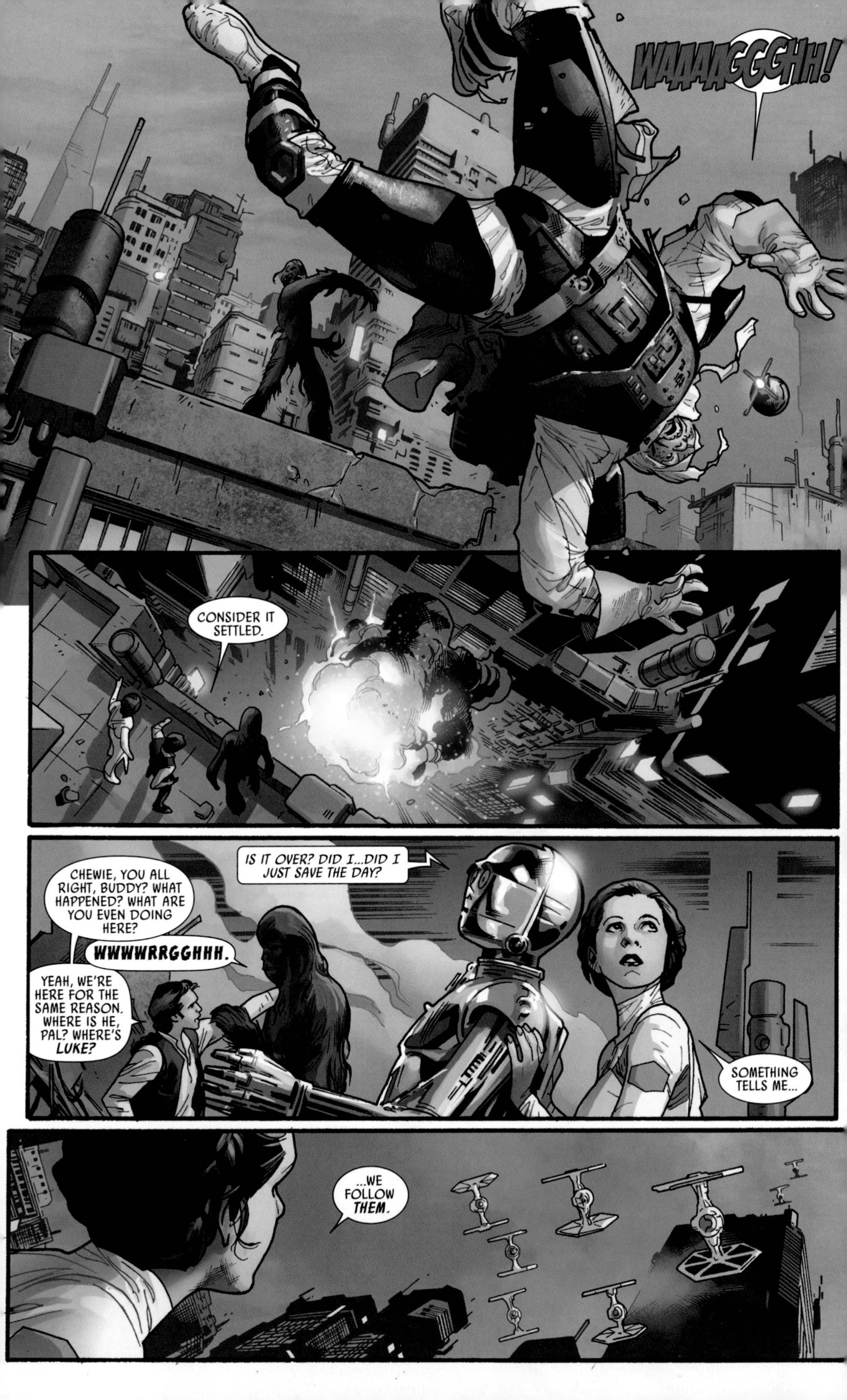
WAAAAGGGHH!
CONSIDER IT SETTLED.
CHEWIE, YOU ALL RIGHT, BUDDY? WHAT HAPPENED? WHAT ARE YOU EVEN DOING HERE?
WWWWRRGGHHH.
YEAH, WE'RE HERE FOR THE SAME REASON. WHERE IS HE, PAL? WHERE'S LUKE?
IS IT OVER? DID I...DID I JUST SAVE THE DAY?
SOMETHING TELLS ME...
...WE FOLLOW THEM.

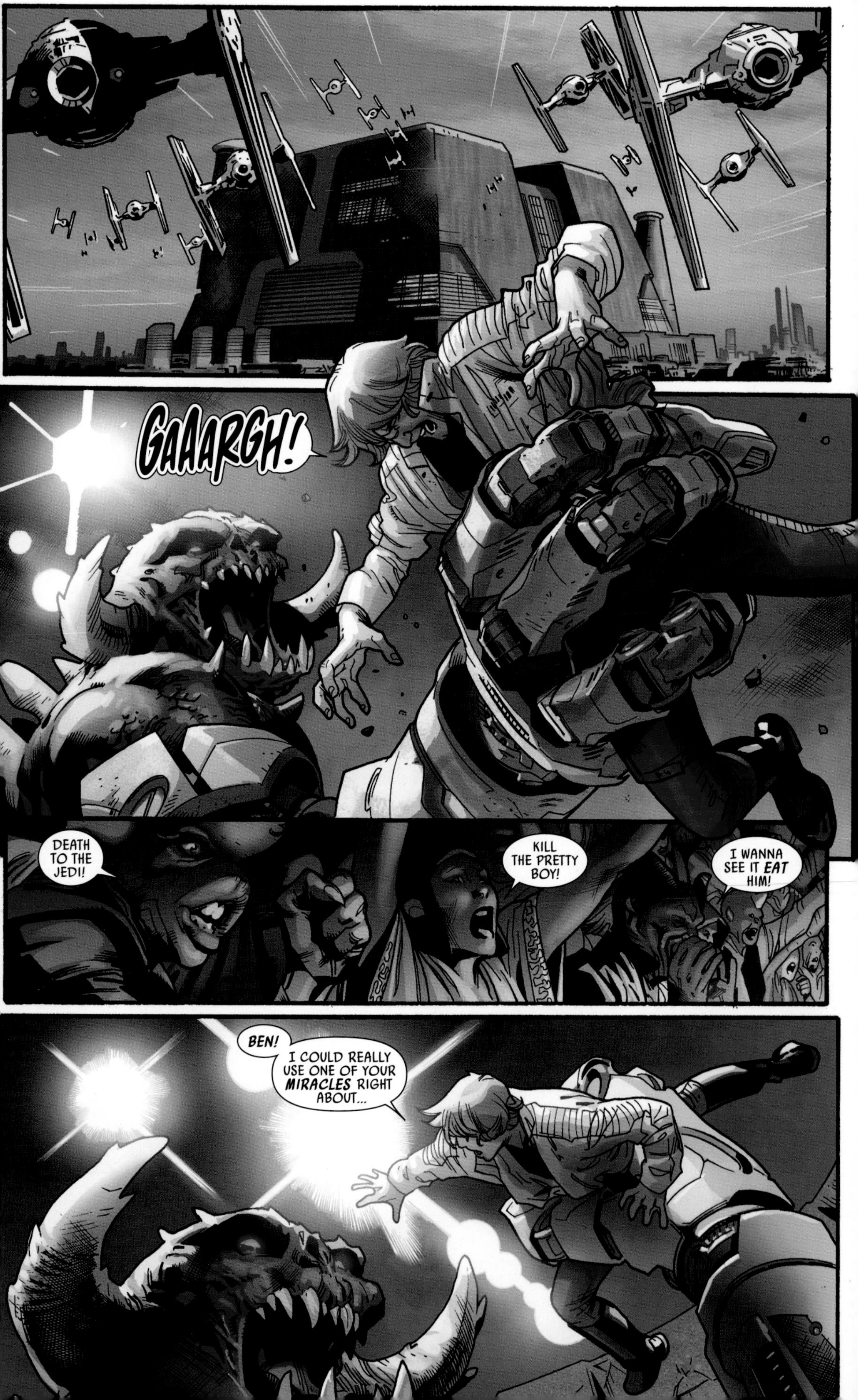
GAAARGH!
DEATH TO THE JEDI!
KILL THE PRETTY BOY!
I WANNA SEE IT EAT HIM!
BEN!
I COULD REALLY USE ONE OF YOUR MIRACLES RIGHT ABOUT...

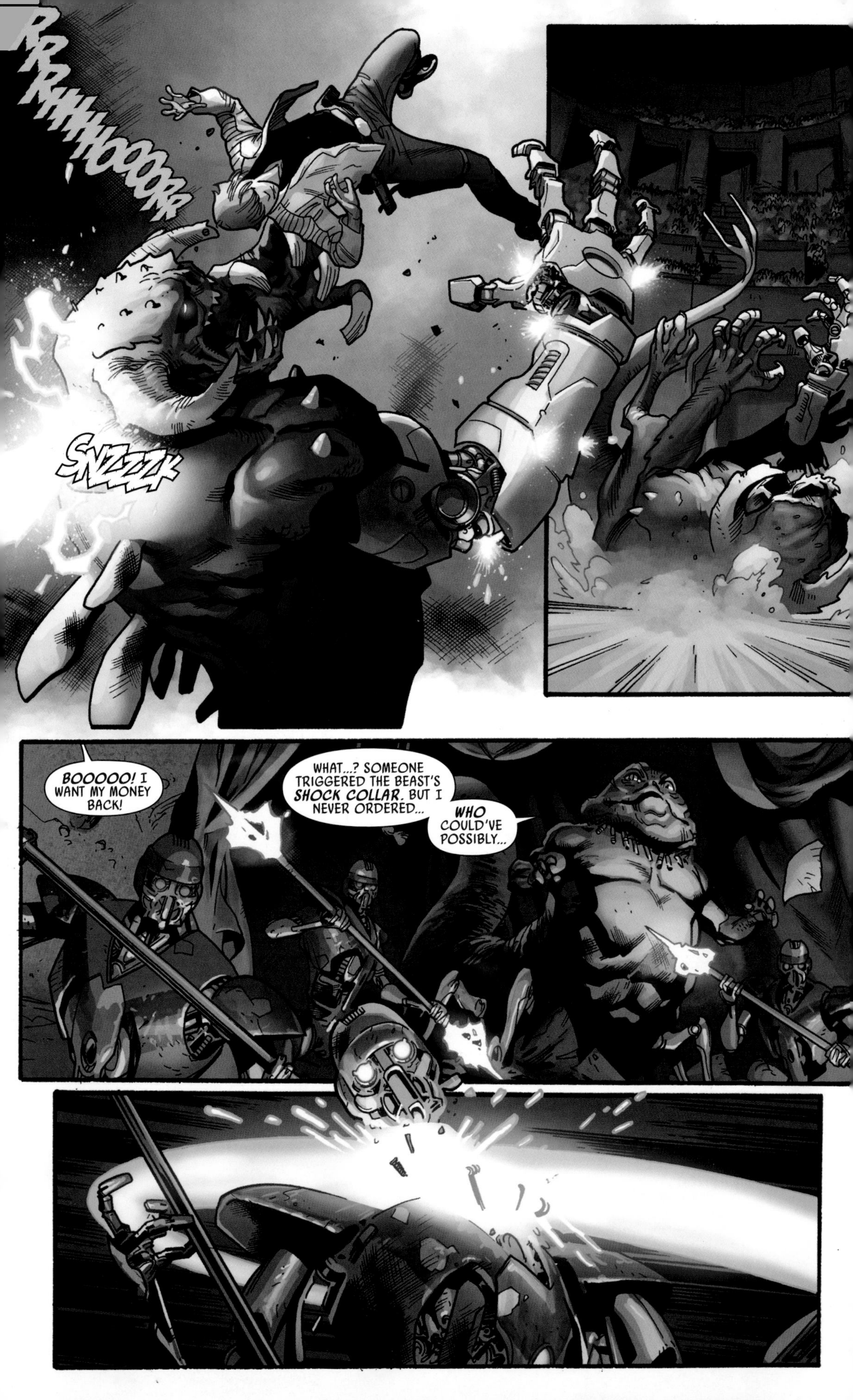
RRRHHHOOOORR
SNZZZK
BOOOOO! I WANT MY MONEY BACK!
WHAT...? SOMEONE TRIGGERED THE BEAST'S SHOCK COLLAR. BUT I NEVER ORDERED...
WHO COULD'VE POSSIBLY...

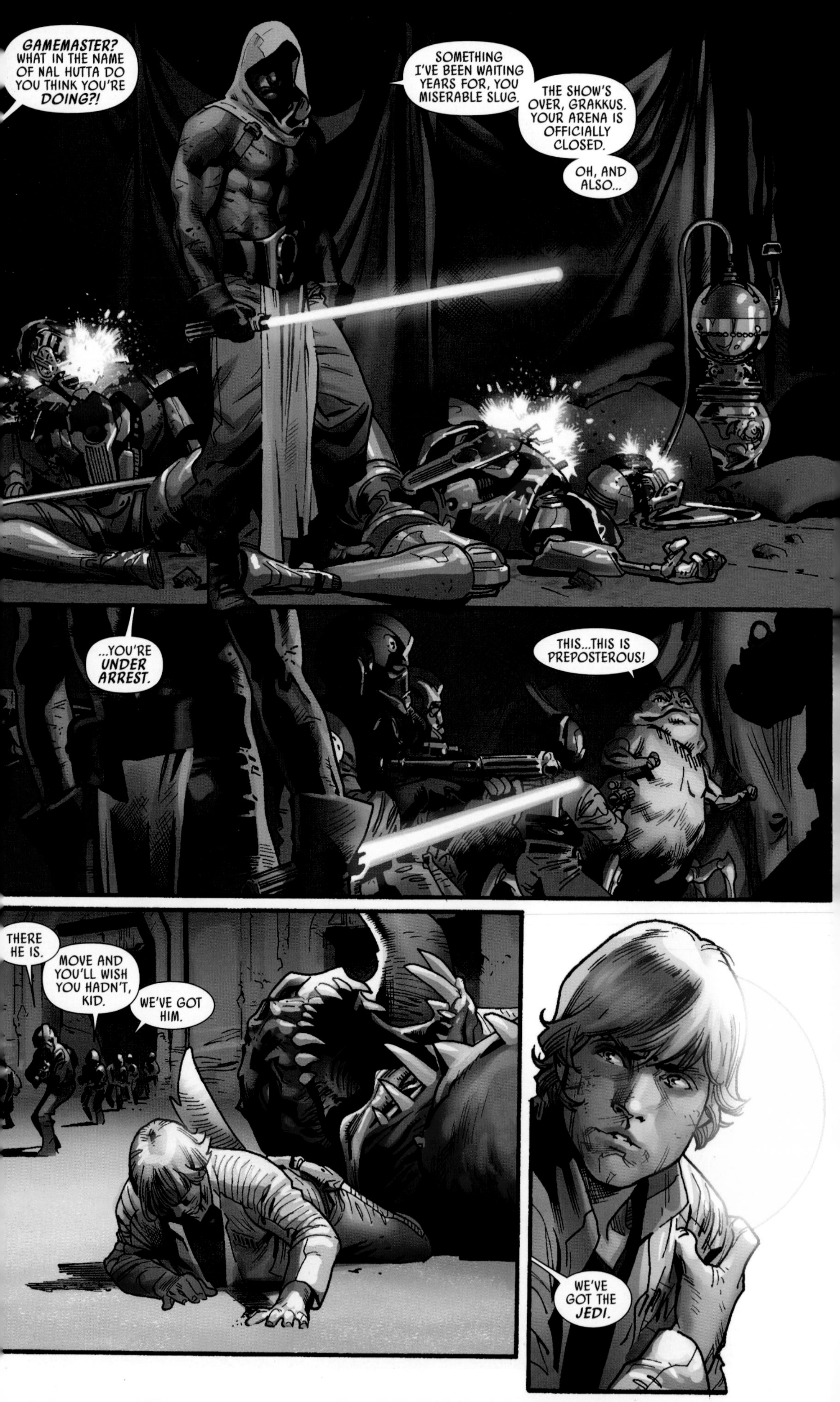

GAMEMASTER? WHAT IN THE NAME OF NAL HUTTA DO YOU THINK YOU'RE DOING?!
SOMETHING I'VE BEEN WAITING YEARS FOR, YOU MISERABLE SLUG.
THE SHOW'S OVER, GRAKKUS. YOUR ARENA IS OFFICIALLY CLOSED.
OH, AND ALSO...
...YOU'RE UNDER ARREST.
THIS...THIS IS PREPOSTEROUS!
THERE HE IS.
MOVE AND YOU'LL WISH YOU HADN'T, KID.
WE'VE GOT HIM.
WE'VE GOT THE JEDI.

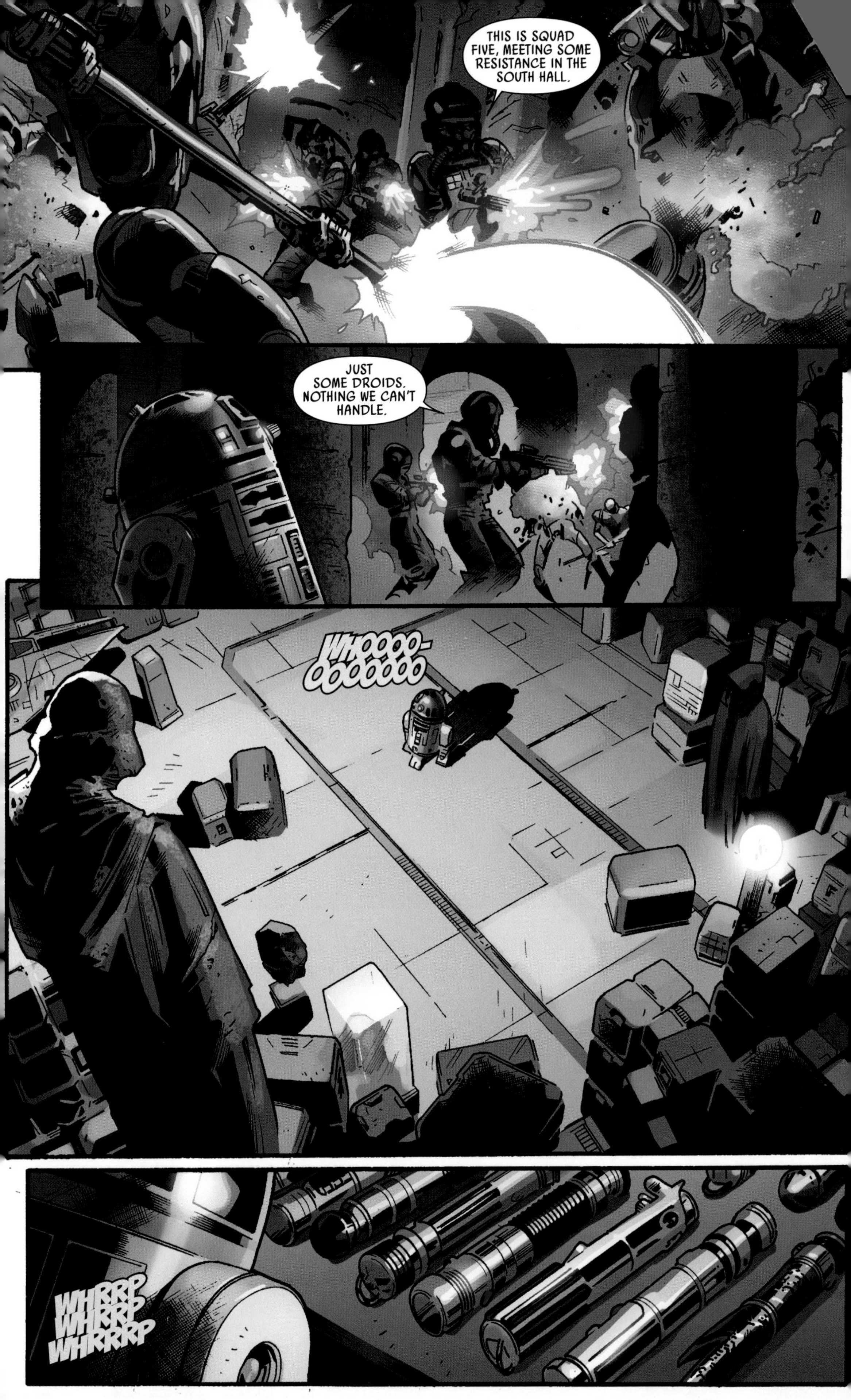
THIS IS SQUAD FIVE, MEETING SOME RESISTANCE IN THE SOUTH HALL.
JUST SOME DROIDS. NOTHING WE CAN'T HANDLE.
WHOOOO-OOOOOOO
WHRRP WHRRP WHRRRP

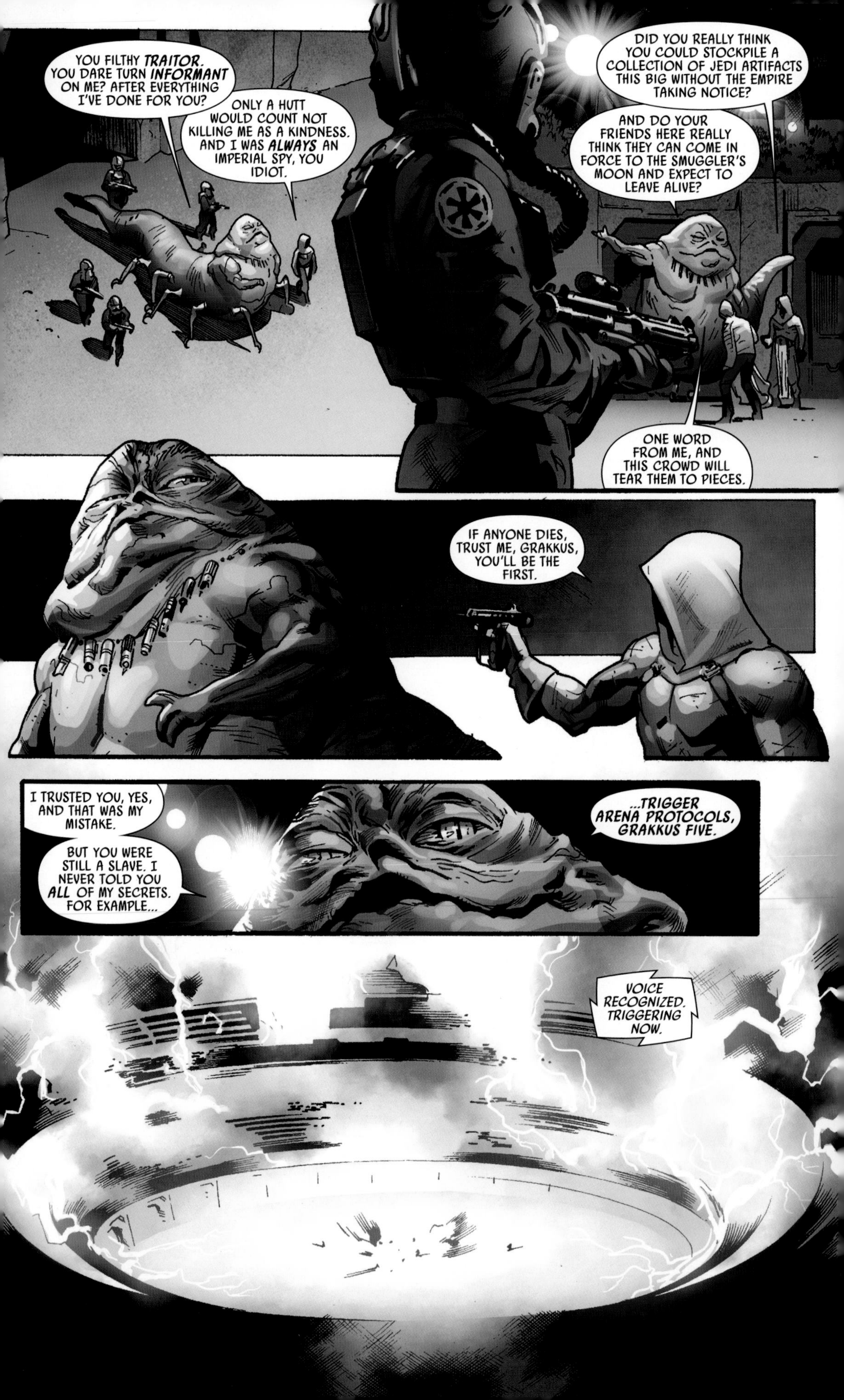
YOU FILTHY TRAITOR. YOU DARE TURN INFORMANT ON ME? AFTER EVERYTHING I'VE DONE FOR YOU?
ONLY A HUTT WOULD COUNT NOT KILLING ME AS A KINDNESS. AND I WAS ALWAYS AN IMPERIAL SPY, YOU IDIOT.
DID YOU REALLY THINK YOU COULD STOCKPILE A COLLECTION OF JEDI ARTIFACTS THIS BIG WITHOUT THE EMPIRE TAKING NOTICE?
AND DO YOUR FRIENDS HERE REALLY THINK THEY CAN COME IN FORCE TO THE SMUGGLER'S MOON AND EXPECT TO LEAVE ALIVE?
ONE WORD FROM ME, AND THIS CROWD WILL TEAR THEM TO PIECES.
IF ANYONE DIES, TRUST ME, GRAKKUS, YOU'LL BE THE FIRST.
I TRUSTED YOU, YES, AND THAT WAS MY MISTAKE.
BUT YOU WERE STILL A SLAVE. I NEVER TOLD YOU ALL OF MY SECRETS. FOR EXAMPLE...
...TRIGGER ARENA PROTOCOLS, GRAKKUS FIVE.
VOICE RECOGNIZED. TRIGGERING NOW.

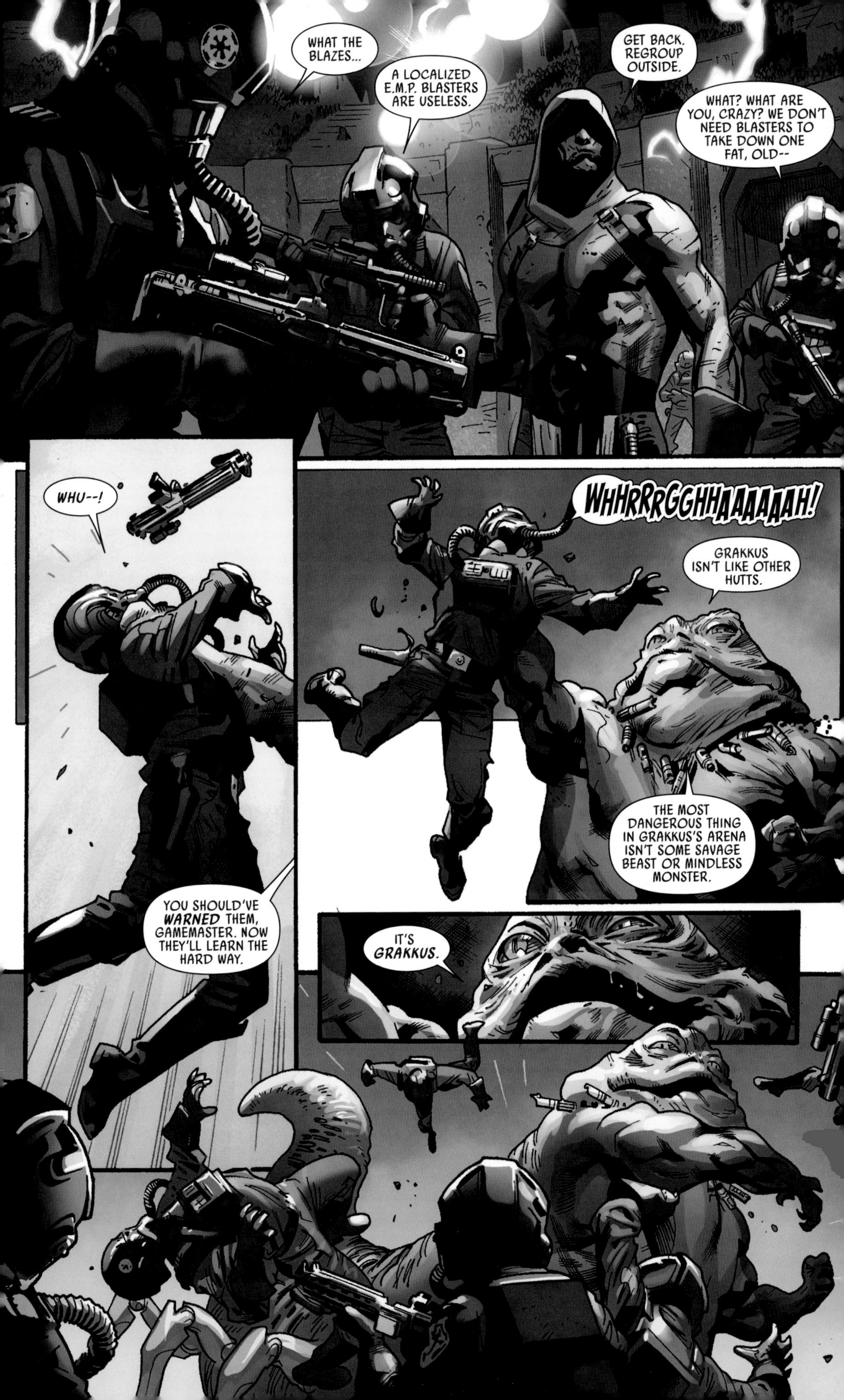
WHAT THE BLAZES...
A LOCALIZED E.M.P. BLASTERS ARE USELESS.
GET BACK. REGROUP OUTSIDE.
WHAT? WHAT ARE YOU, CRAZY? WE DON'T NEED BLASTERS TO TAKE DOWN ONE FAT, OLD--
WHU--!
YOU SHOULD'VE WARNED THEM, GAMEMASTER. NOW THEY'LL LEARN THE HARD WAY.
WHHRRRGGHHAAAAAAH!
GRAKKUS ISN'T LIKE OTHER HUTTS.
THE MOST DANGEROUS THING IN GRAKKUS'S ARENA ISN'T SOME SAVAGE BEAST OR MINDLESS MONSTER.
IT'S GRAKKUS.

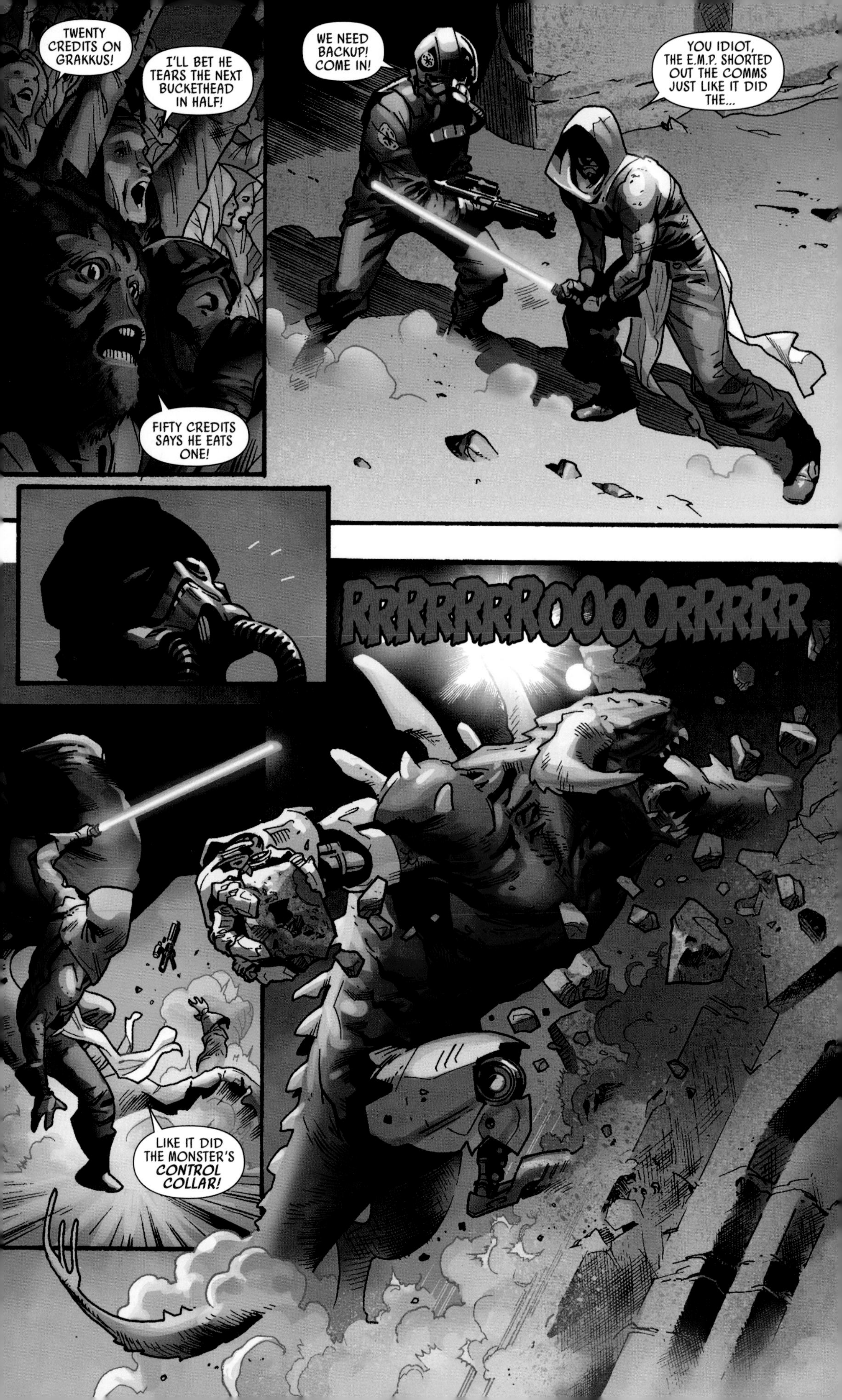
TWENTY CREDITS ON GRAKKUS!
I'LL BET HE TEARS THE NEXT BUCKETHEAD IN HALF!
FIFTY CREDITS SAYS HE EATS ONE!
WE NEED BACKUP! COME IN!
YOU IDIOT, THE E.M.P. SHORTED OUT THE COMMS JUST LIKE IT DID THE...
RRRRRRRROOOOORRRRR
LIKE IT DID THE MONSTER'S CONTROL COLLAR!

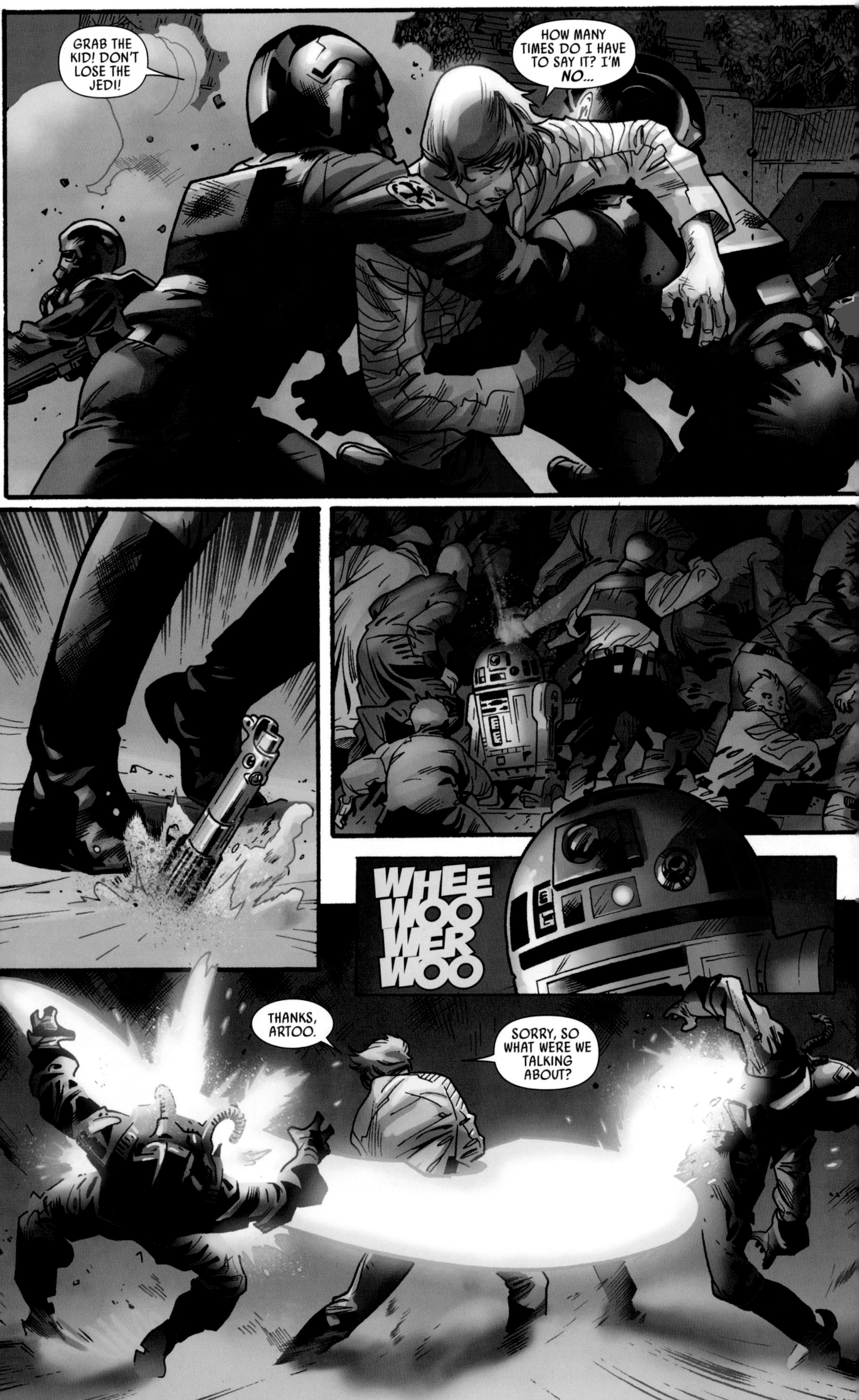
GRAB THE KID! DON'T LOSE THE JEDI!
HOW MANY TIMES DO I HAVE TO SAY IT? I'M NO...
WHEE WOO WER WOO
THANKS, ARTOO.
SORRY, SO WHAT WERE WE TALKING ABOUT?

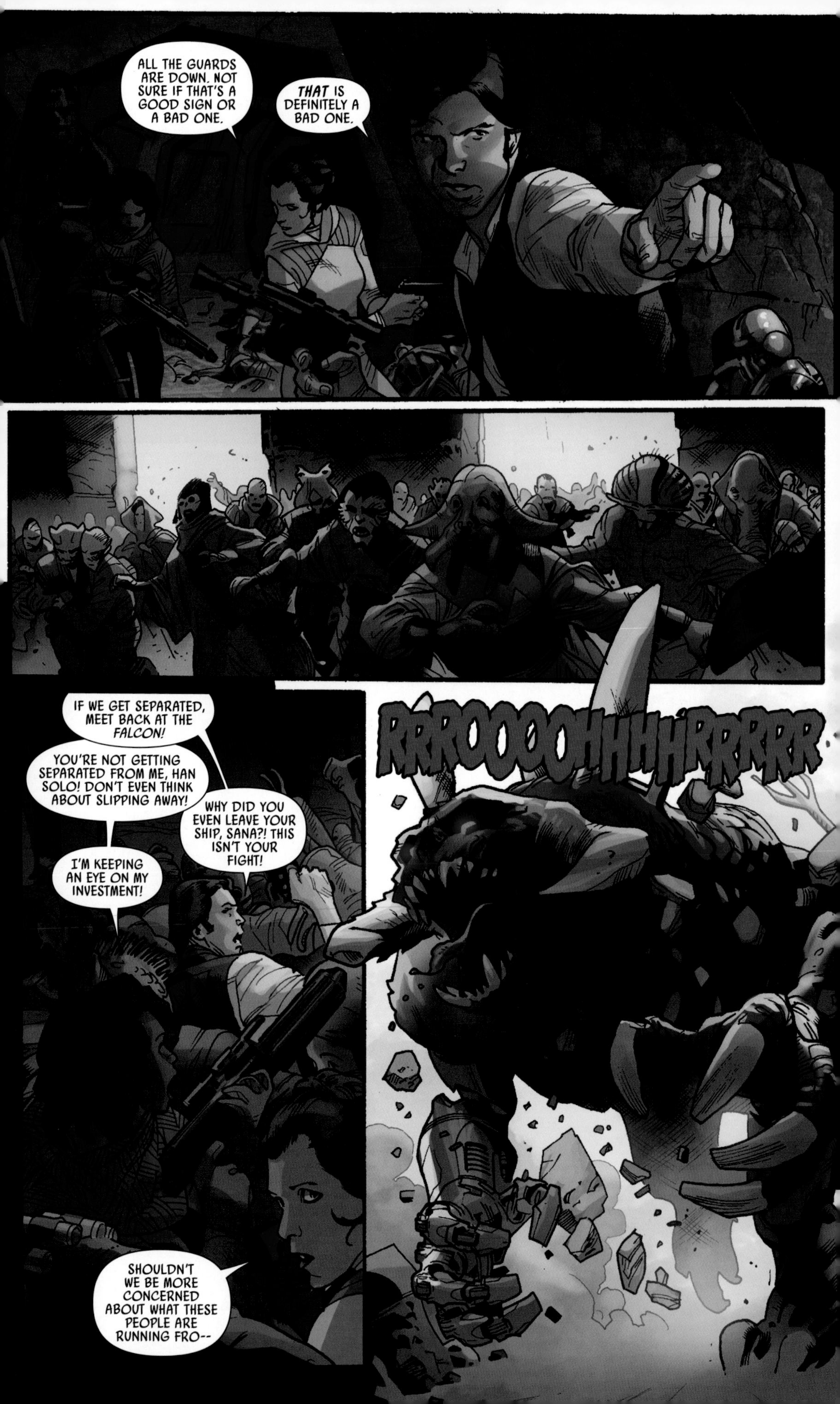
ALL THE GUARDS ARE DOWN. NOT SURE IF THAT'S A GOOD SIGN OR A BAD ONE.
THAT IS DEFINITELY A BAD ONE.
IF WE GET SEPARATED, MEET BACK AT THE *FALCON!*
YOU'RE NOT GETTING SEPARATED FROM ME, HAN SOLO! DON'T EVEN THINK ABOUT SLIPPING AWAY!
WHY DID YOU EVEN LEAVE YOUR SHIP, SANA?! THIS ISN'T YOUR FIGHT!
I'M KEEPING AN EYE ON MY INVESTMENT!
SHOULDN'T WE BE MORE CONCERNED ABOUT WHAT THESE PEOPLE ARE RUNNING FRO--
RRROOOOOHHHHRRRRR

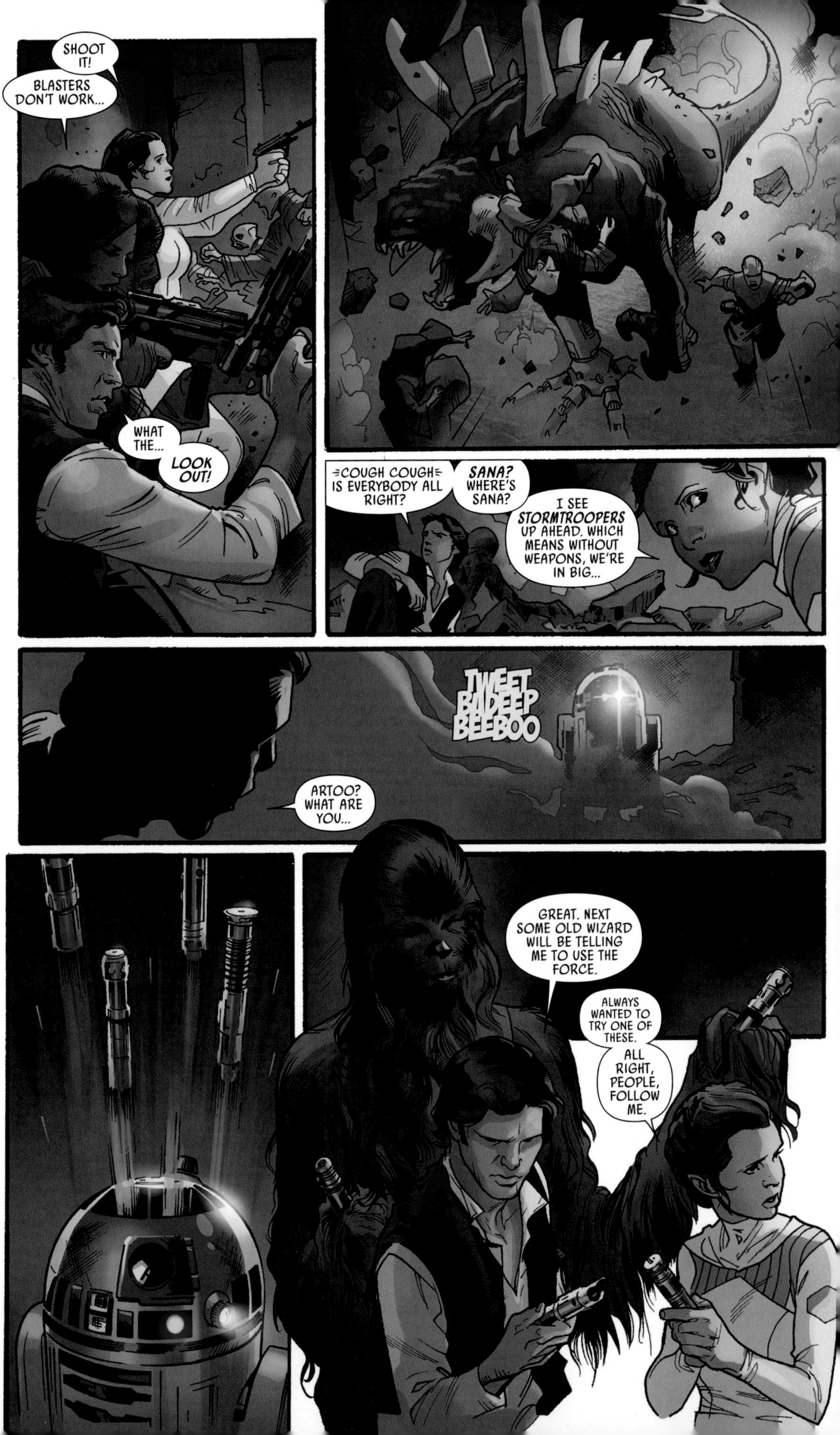
SHOOT IT!
BLASTERS DON'T WORK...
WHAT THE... LOOK OUT!
≈COUGH COUGH≈ IS EVERYBODY ALL RIGHT?
SANA? WHERE'S SANA?
I SEE STORMTROOPERS UP AHEAD. WHICH MEANS WITHOUT WEAPONS, WE'RE IN BIG...
TWEET BADEEP BEEBOO
ARTOO? WHAT ARE YOU...
GREAT. NEXT SOME OLD WIZARD WILL BE TELLING ME TO USE THE FORCE.
ALWAYS WANTED TO TRY ONE OF THESE.
ALL RIGHT, PEOPLE, FOLLOW ME.

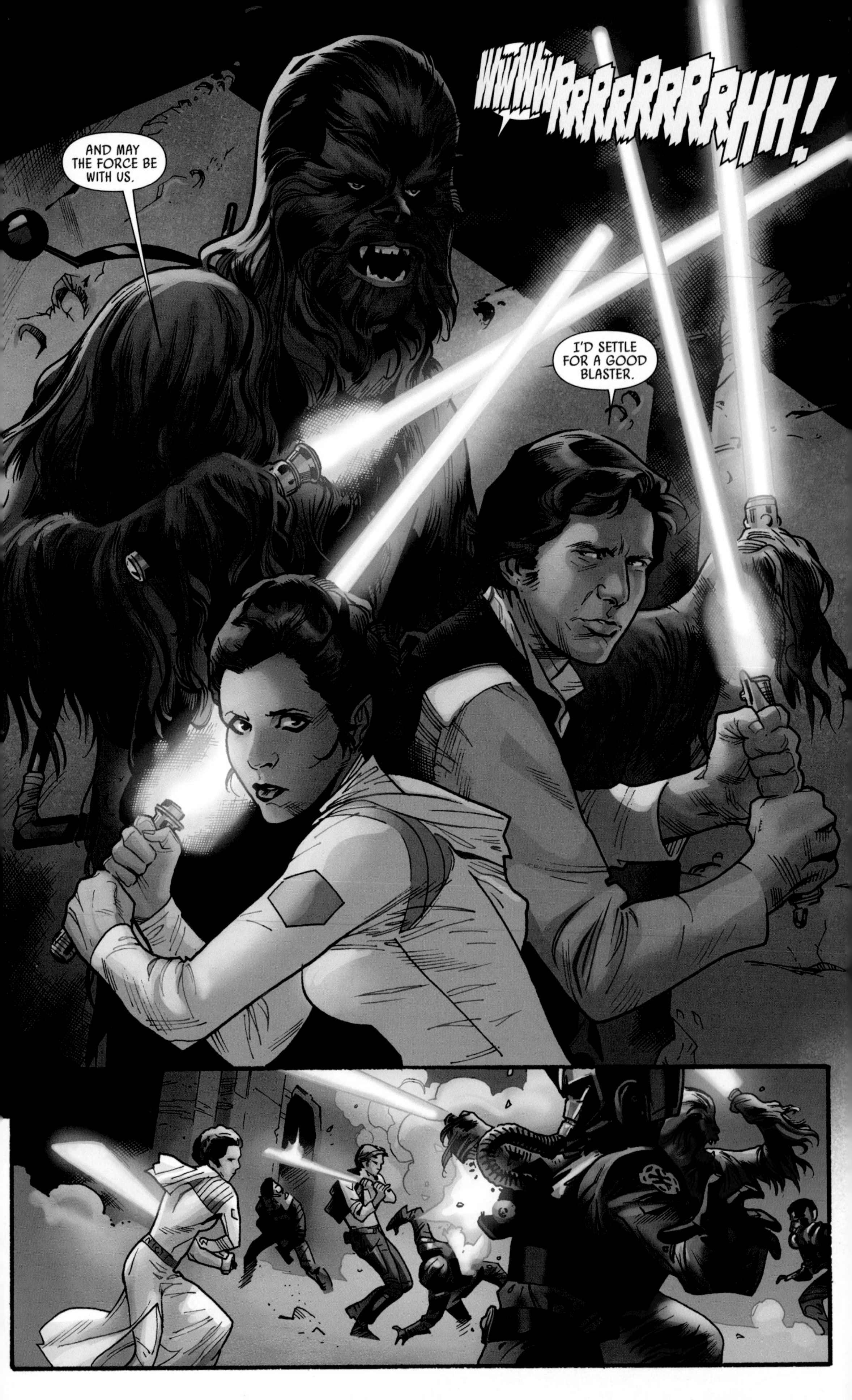
WWWWWRRRRRRRRRHH!
AND MAY THE FORCE BE WITH US.
I'D SETTLE FOR A GOOD BLASTER.

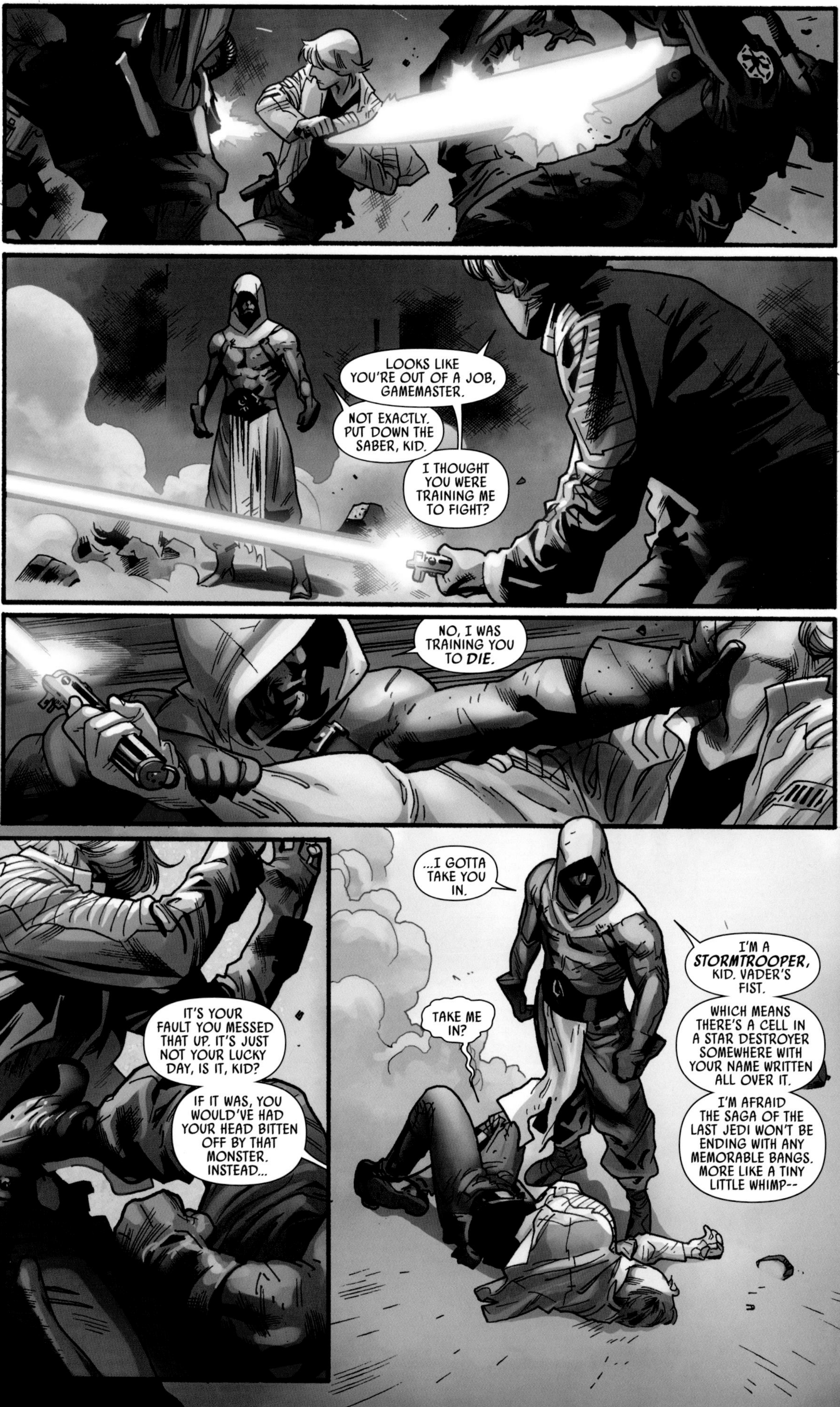
LOOKS LIKE YOU'RE OUT OF A JOB, GAMEMASTER.
NOT EXACTLY. PUT DOWN THE SABER, KID.
I THOUGHT YOU WERE TRAINING ME TO FIGHT?
NO, I WAS TRAINING YOU TO *DIE.*
IT'S YOUR FAULT YOU MESSED THAT UP. IT'S JUST NOT YOUR LUCKY DAY, IS IT, KID?
IF IT WAS, YOU WOULD'VE HAD YOUR HEAD BITTEN OFF BY THAT MONSTER. INSTEAD...
...I GOTTA TAKE YOU IN.
TAKE ME IN?
I'M A *STORMTROOPER,* KID. VADER'S FIST.
WHICH MEANS THERE'S A CELL IN A STAR DESTROYER SOMEWHERE WITH YOUR NAME WRITTEN ALL OVER IT.
I'M AFRAID THE SAGA OF THE LAST JEDI WON'T BE ENDING WITH ANY MEMORABLE BANGS. MORE LIKE A TINY LITTLE WHIMP--

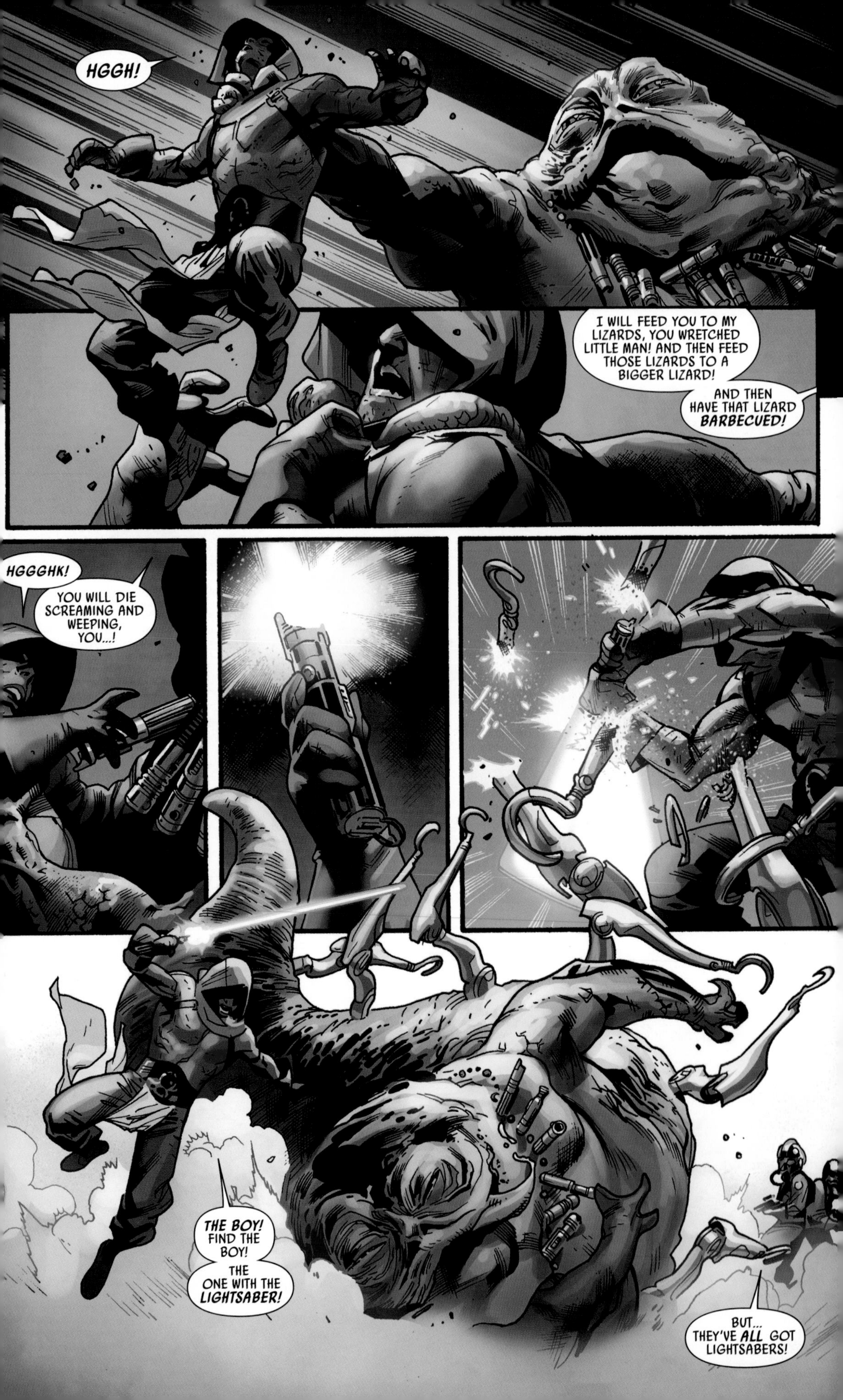
HGGH!
I WILL FEED YOU TO MY LIZARDS, YOU WRETCHED LITTLE MAN! AND THEN FEED THOSE LIZARDS TO A BIGGER LIZARD!
AND THEN HAVE THAT LIZARD BARBECUED!
HGGGHK!
YOU WILL DIE SCREAMING AND WEEPING, YOU...!
THE BOY! FIND THE BOY!
THE ONE WITH THE LIGHTSABER!
BUT... THEY'VE ALL GOT LIGHTSABERS!

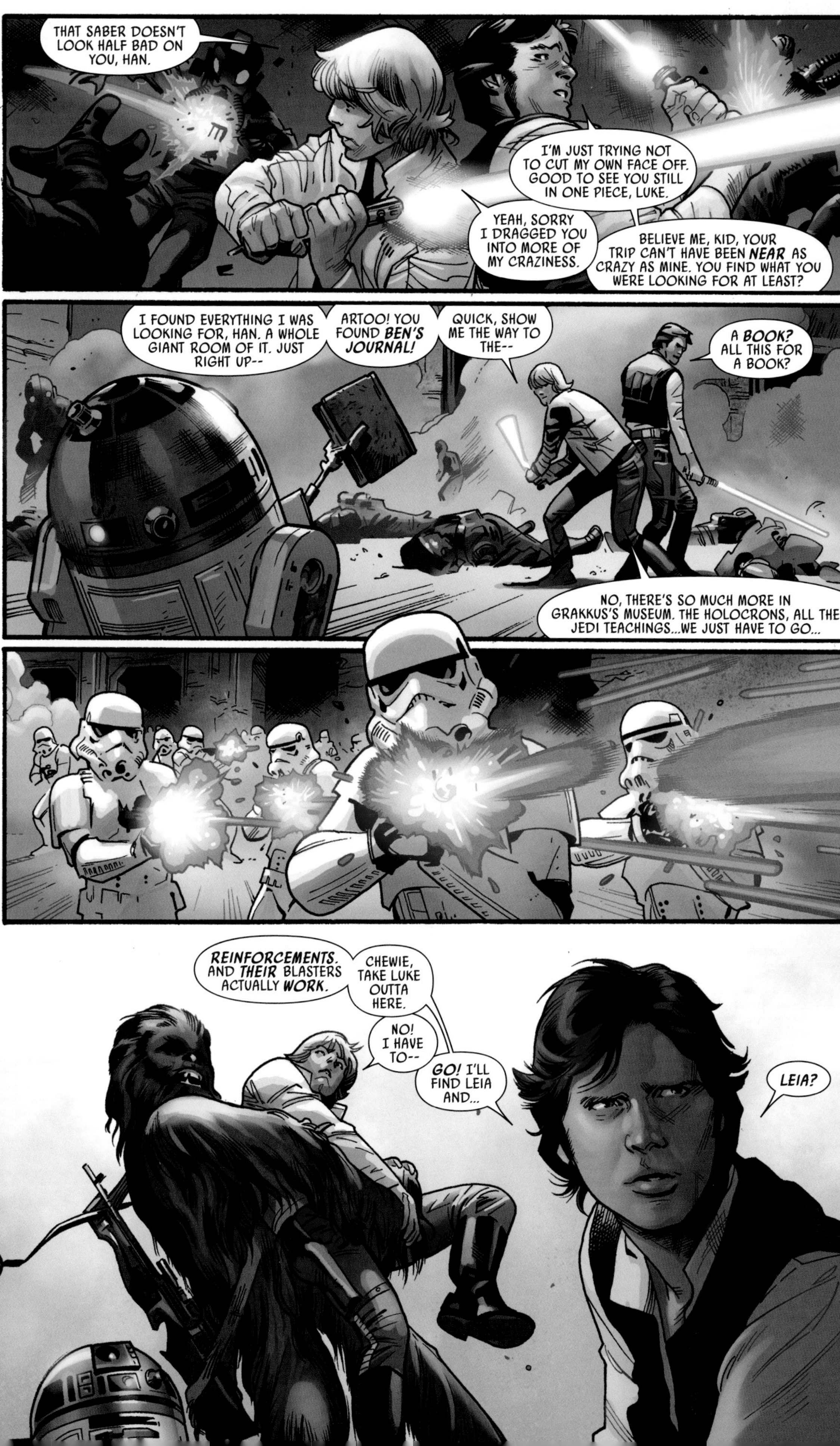
THAT SABER DOESN'T LOOK HALF BAD ON YOU, HAN.
I'M JUST TRYING NOT TO CUT MY OWN FACE OFF. GOOD TO SEE YOU STILL IN ONE PIECE, LUKE.
YEAH, SORRY I DRAGGED YOU INTO MORE OF MY CRAZINESS.
BELIEVE ME, KID, YOUR TRIP CAN'T HAVE BEEN NEAR AS CRAZY AS MINE. YOU FIND WHAT YOU WERE LOOKING FOR AT LEAST?
I FOUND EVERYTHING I WAS LOOKING FOR, HAN. A WHOLE GIANT ROOM OF IT. JUST RIGHT UP--
ARTOO! YOU FOUND BEN'S JOURNAL!
QUICK, SHOW ME THE WAY TO THE--
A BOOK? ALL THIS FOR A BOOK?
NO, THERE'S SO MUCH MORE IN GRAKKUS'S MUSEUM. THE HOLOCRONS, ALL THE JEDI TEACHINGS...WE JUST HAVE TO GO...
REINFORCEMENTS. AND THEIR BLASTERS ACTUALLY WORK.
CHEWIE, TAKE LUKE OUTTA HERE.
NO! I HAVE TO--
GO! I'LL FIND LEIA AND...
LEIA?

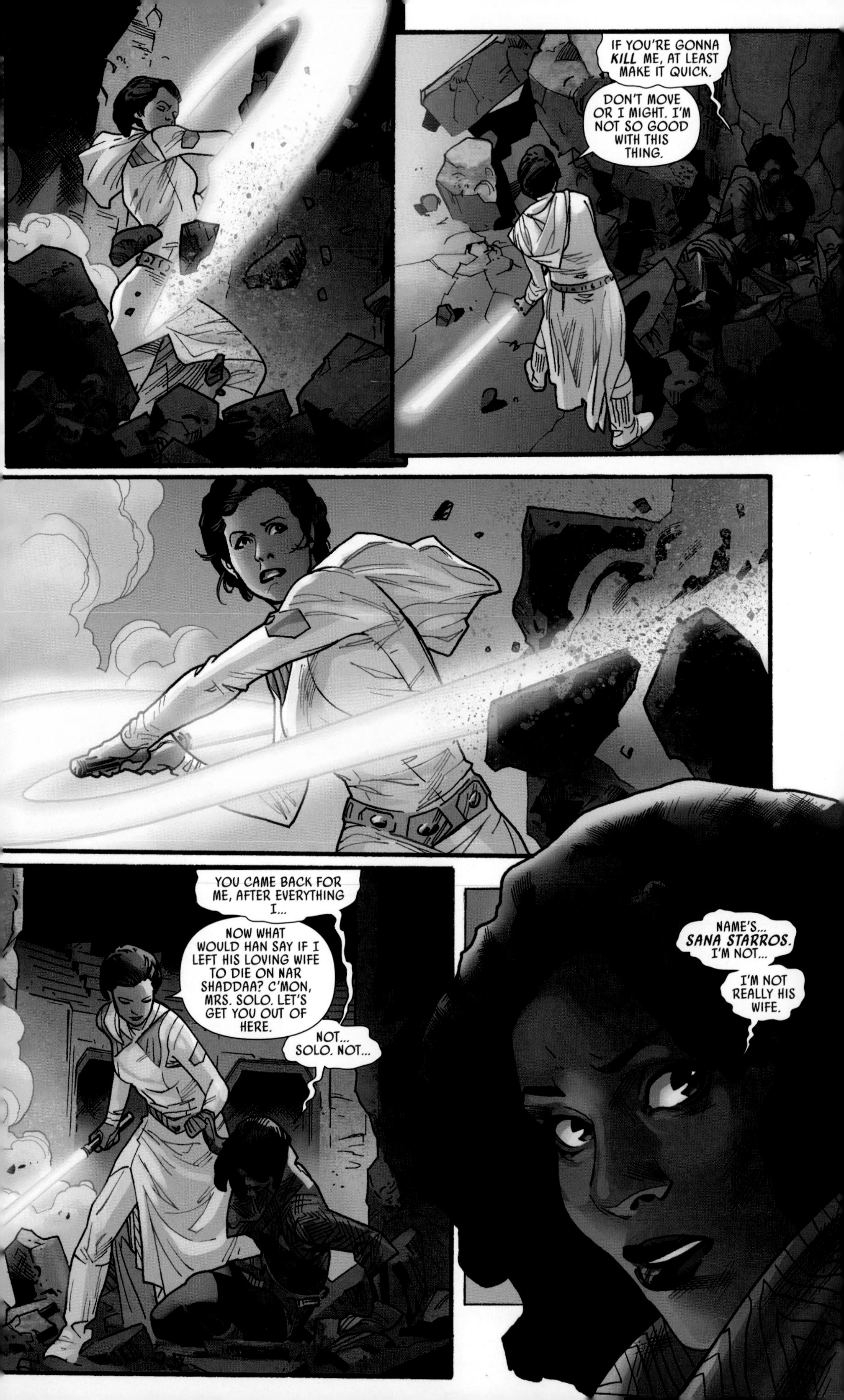
IF YOU'RE GONNA KILL ME, AT LEAST MAKE IT QUICK.
DON'T MOVE OR I MIGHT. I'M NOT SO GOOD WITH THIS THING.
YOU CAME BACK FOR ME, AFTER EVERYTHING I...
NOW WHAT WOULD HAN SAY IF I LEFT HIS LOVING WIFE TO DIE ON NAR SHADDAA? C'MON, MRS. SOLO. LET'S GET YOU OUT OF HERE.
NOT... SOLO. NOT...
NAME'S... SANA STARROS. I'M NOT...
I'M NOT REALLY HIS WIFE.

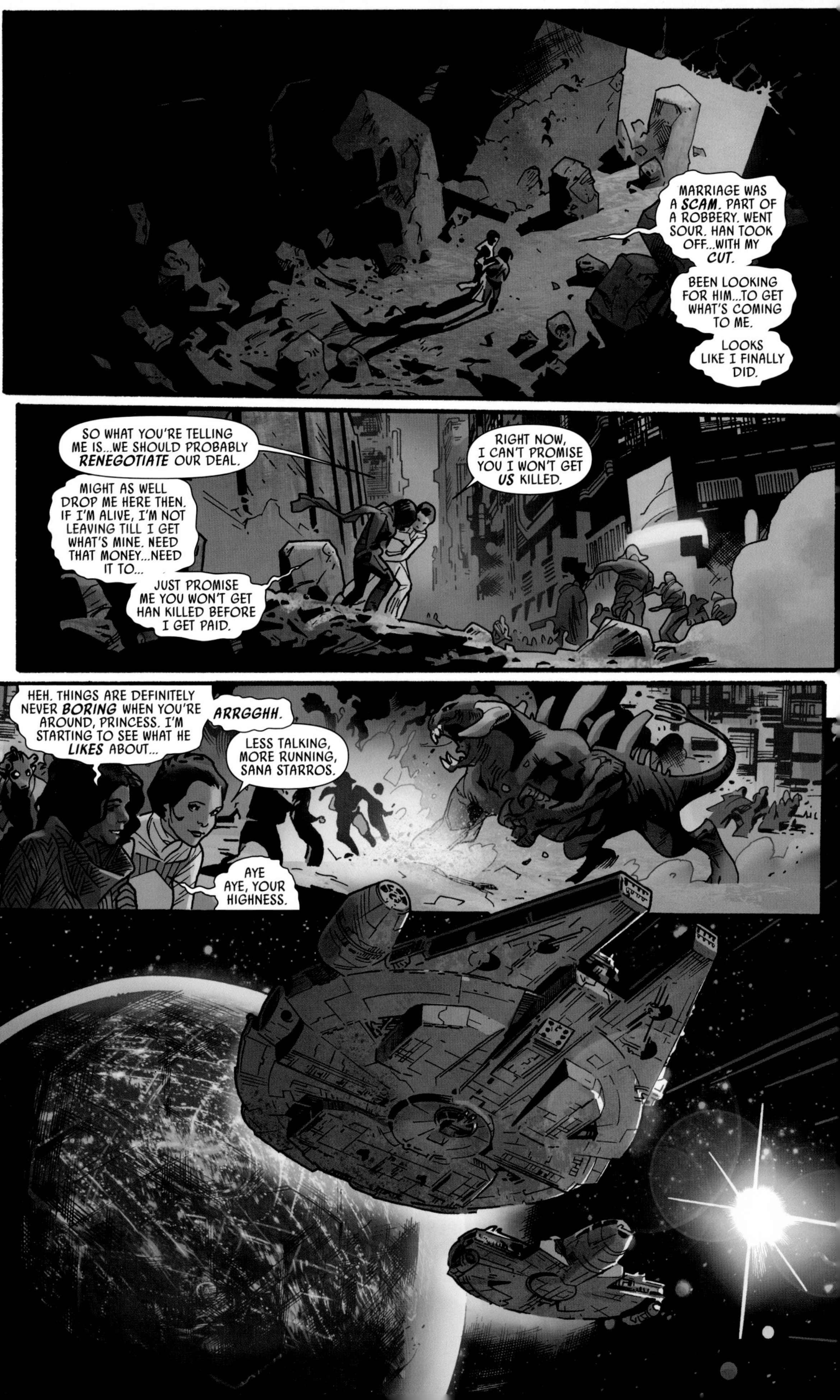
MARRIAGE WAS A SCAM. PART OF A ROBBERY. WENT SOUR. HAN TOOK OFF...WITH MY CUT.
BEEN LOOKING FOR HIM...TO GET WHAT'S COMING TO ME.
LOOKS LIKE I FINALLY DID.
SO WHAT YOU'RE TELLING ME IS...WE SHOULD PROBABLY RENEGOTIATE OUR DEAL.
MIGHT AS WELL DROP ME HERE THEN. IF I'M ALIVE, I'M NOT LEAVING TILL I GET WHAT'S MINE. NEED THAT MONEY...NEED IT TO...
RIGHT NOW, I CAN'T PROMISE YOU I WON'T GET US KILLED.
JUST PROMISE ME YOU WON'T GET HAN KILLED BEFORE I GET PAID.
HEH. THINGS ARE DEFINITELY NEVER BORING WHEN YOU'RE AROUND, PRINCESS. I'M STARTING TO SEE WHAT HE LIKES ABOUT...
ARRGGHH.
LESS TALKING, MORE RUNNING, SANA STARROS.
AYE AYE, YOUR HIGHNESS.

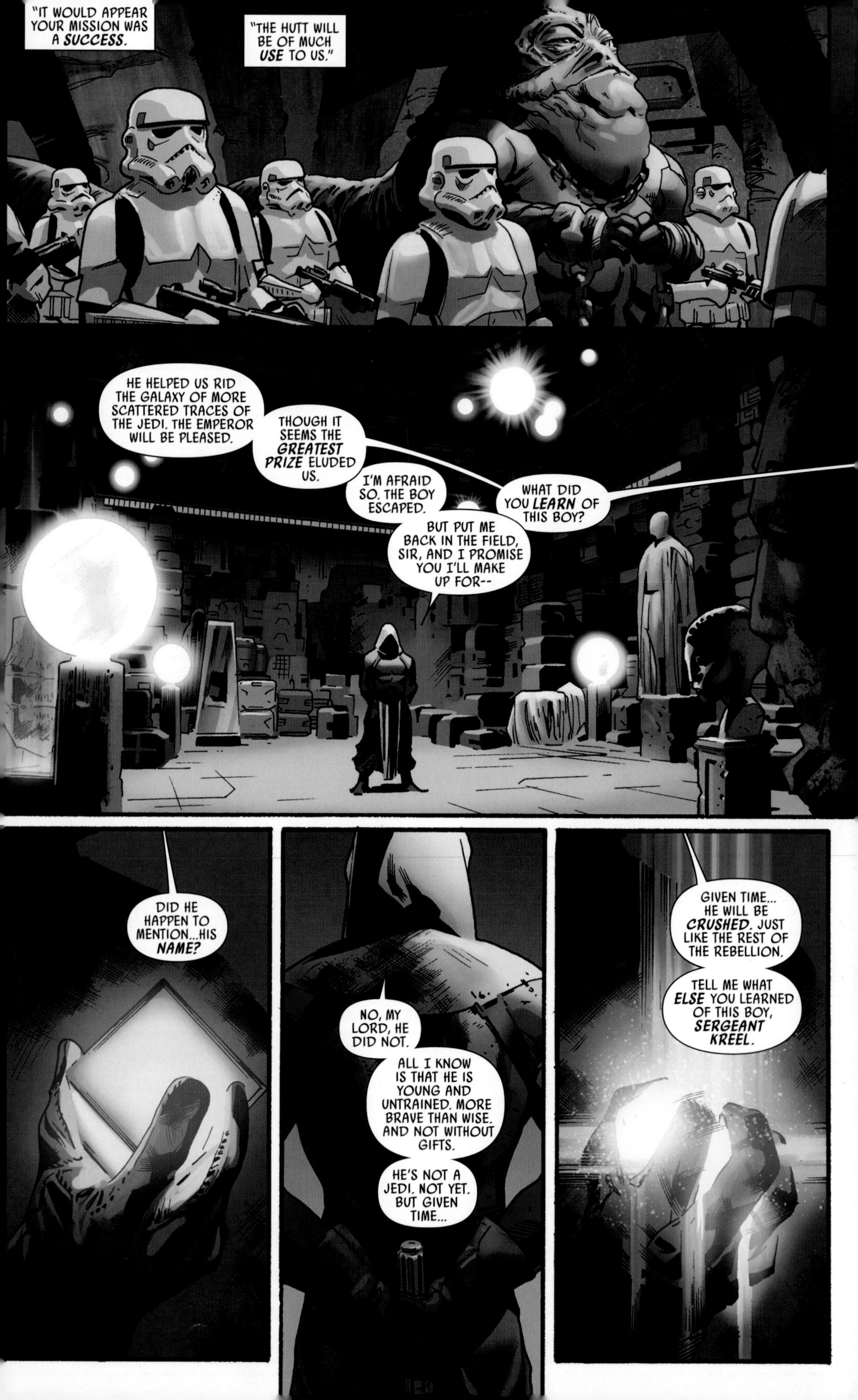
"IT WOULD APPEAR YOUR MISSION WAS A SUCCESS.
"THE HUTT WILL BE OF MUCH USE TO US."
HE HELPED US RID THE GALAXY OF MORE SCATTERED TRACES OF THE JEDI. THE EMPEROR WILL BE PLEASED.
THOUGH IT SEEMS THE GREATEST PRIZE ELUDED US.
I'M AFRAID SO. THE BOY ESCAPED.
WHAT DID YOU LEARN OF THIS BOY?
BUT PUT ME BACK IN THE FIELD, SIR, AND I PROMISE YOU I'LL MAKE UP FOR--
DID HE HAPPEN TO MENTION...HIS NAME?
NO, MY LORD, HE DID NOT.
ALL I KNOW IS THAT HE IS YOUNG AND UNTRAINED. MORE BRAVE THAN WISE. AND NOT WITHOUT GIFTS.
HE'S NOT A JEDI. NOT YET. BUT GIVEN TIME...
GIVEN TIME... HE WILL BE CRUSHED. JUST LIKE THE REST OF THE REBELLION.
TELL ME WHAT ELSE YOU LEARNED OF THIS BOY, SERGEANT KREEL.

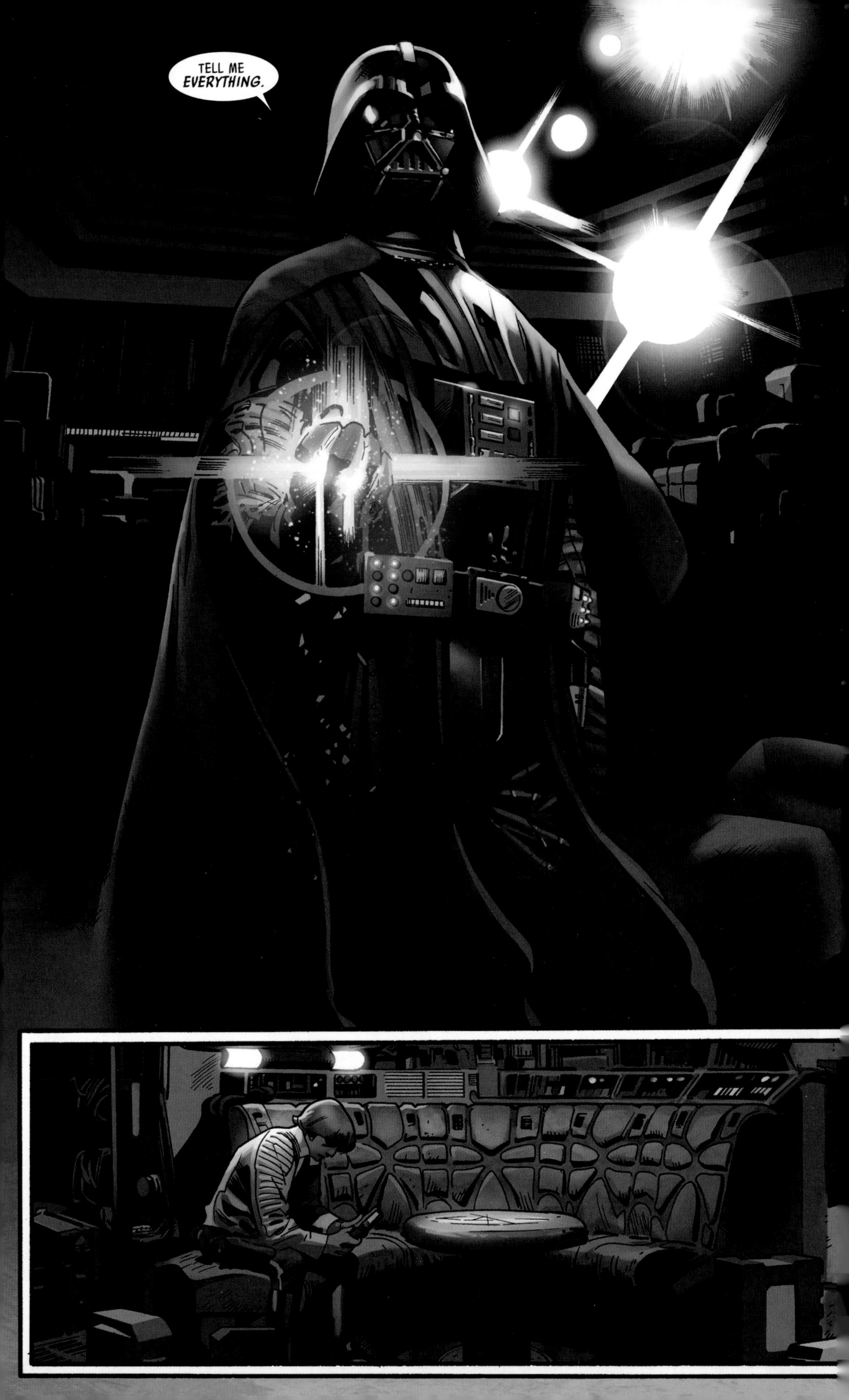
TELL ME *EVERYTHING.*